By B. S. H. Garcia

The Heart of Quinaria

FROM THE
ASHES

THE HEART OF QUINARIA NOVELETTE

B. S. H. GARCIA

First edition: May 2023

Cover design by MIBLART

Silhouette art by Jared Garcia

Interior design by B. S. H. Garcia

ISBN 979-8-9867208-4-5 (hardback)
ISBN 979-8-9867208-2-1 (paperback)

www.bshgarcia.com

LOST RELIC

For Kaylea.

CONTENTS

Believe nothing you hear, and only one half that you see.

—Edgar Allan Poe

IGTHEOS

D eath, or defeat. The options loomed over Igtheos like
starved ravager birds waiting for their prey to succumb
to whatever illness or predator had befallen them.

Death was honorable. To avoid surrender in the face of certain failure was the sort of heroic tale that inspired generations
to come, driving future peoples to action when their very rights
to existence were threatened. It meant that, even if solely in
principle, their little rebellion won.

Death was also stupid. Too many lives to gamble with, too
many bloodlines forever shattered by a leader's arrogance. The
great tales never discussed the true cost of heroism, the innocents sacrificed to make a point.

But what if they were willing? Did they want this, too, all
the men and women who had stood by him these two years,
trusting that their defiance would result in some semblance of
justice? Or perhaps they were tired, ready to surrender, but too
ashamed to admit it.

Igtheos groaned as he pressed away from the suffocating pil-
lows of the lounge chair. The quills poked through the thin silk
that contained them and did little to relieve his aches—physi-
cally or psychologically. Even if they had offered him comfort,
he didn't deserve it. Not while his soldiers and those loyal to
him suffered long watches, cold nights, and food shortages. He
was no exception to the latter. Stomach rumbling, he trod the

marble floors to where a thin curtain separated the room from
a balcony overlooking a city under siege. Smoke curled into
the bloodred sunset. A handful of rebels worked to quench the
flames near the south wall where Ashaat's army had launched
their latest volley of fire arrows. The damage was minimal;
Ashaat cared much for the great city he strove to conquer, and
the fortified walls were all but impenetrable.

It was all for show, anyway. There were other ways to win
a war, and Ashaat, ever in search of a spectacle, preferred
non-conventional methods whenever possible. The infrequent
attacks and occasional deathstalker flyovers were merely re-
minders that Igtheos and his followers were prisoners in their
stronghold, easily outnumbered, should they dare to leave. And
their food had all but run out.

Igtheos tightened the sash around his linen tunic as he returned to the bedroom. He glared at the finely etched pillars, the
silken tapestries running from ceiling to floor, the unlit fire pots
embossed with gold. A palace fit for a ruler as hollow as its halls.
Originally constructed as an institution for learning, it had since
transformed into an exclusive gathering place for the nation's
unelected public servants, and, most recently, become the future
home of a self-proclaimed ruler.

The door creaked. Igtheos's hand flew to his dagger.

A face appeared in the shadows, illuminated by the soft green
glow of a nevethium crystal no larger than a pea. The wearer
touched her necklace, briefly dousing the room in darkness.

"Do you often brood in the shadows while I'm away?"

Igtheos took a step toward her. "My lady, the shadows are all
that exist in your absence."

She removed her hand from the crystal, once again illumi-
nating the room in green ambiance. The corner of her lip curled
upward. "Is that what you tell all your lovers?"

"Only the ones I wed."

"Lucky me." She closed the distance between them, placed one hand on his chest, and ran the other over his bare head with warm, ink-stained fingers. "I like it," she whispered, her green eyes flashing. "But without those telling white locks, how will others infer your elevated status from a distance?"

"It's becoming of the leader of a human rebellion to sacrifice some privileges." He wrapped an arm around her waist, breathing in her scent, a mixture of honey and sun-blood blossoms.

"I thought that was my job as the alluring human wife of a nyrian. Makes quite an effective political statement, even without Zaria's existence."

"And is our sweet miracle asleep?"

"Is that what you call the little tyrant?"

"It's you she takes after."

Elize raised an eyebrow.

"Every bit as beautiful as her mother." Igtheos leaned in until his lips hovered just above hers.

"Clever man."

The moonlight softened her already smooth features, highlighted the freckles on her nose. Igtheos untied her travel cloak. It slithered to the floor, exposing waves of hair as red and free as the Tsabian Desert. Elize pulled him close, kissing him long and slow, her fingers running across the back of his head, down his neck and back. Her hand slipped into his sash, and he froze, remembering what he'd tucked inside it.

"What's this?" she asked, sliding the message free.

Igtheos made to grab it from her, but she danced just out of his reach and held the parchment up to the moonlight. The smile melted from her face as she rubbed her thumb over the broken wax seal.

"Ashaat sent you this?"

"Elize, give it here."

She stormed past him and retrieved a piece of flint from the bedside. "What does he want now? Have years of senseless bloodshed not yet quenched his lust for war?"

"Let's just enjoy tonight, please." Igtheos sat on the bed to remove his sandals as she lit a fire pot. "I've missed you."

"It's his fault we've been separated." She frowned and unfurled the parchment. "When did you receive this? Why didn't you tell me?"

"I was going to tell you after we had more than five minutes to ourselves," he muttered, not that she was listening, given the increasingly souring expression on her face.

Igtheos sank into the bed, his gaze tracing the embroidered swirls on the underside of the canopy for what felt like an eternity. There'd be no love-making tonight. Once Elize descended into righteous anger, it took her hours—if not days—to crawl back out.

"Well, then."

Igtheos spared her a glance. She stared into the flames, brow furrowed, the parchment crinkling beneath her fingertips. "What are your thoughts on the matter?"

Elize dropped the parchment into the fire. "*This* is my initial thought."

"That's helpful."

If she heard him, she made no effort to acknowledge it. "Does he honestly think I'm just going to hand over the scrolls like that, especially after I went to such great lengths to hide them? He's gone mad."

"He went mad long ago. This, however... " Igtheos gestured to the ash in the fire pot. "This was calculated. He knows he's all but starved us out."

"We fight our way out, then. Utilize the stormbirds."

"It's not that simple, my starlight," he said, shoving off the bed. He felt old, far older than his two hundred and sixty years, far older than its forty-something human equivalent. "We lost too many soldiers in our last push to secure the city, hoping it would force Ashaat's army to retreat long enough for us to recoup. He never accepted the bait." Igtheos wrapped his arms around Elize's waist from behind. She didn't lean into him, but she didn't pull away either. "We've been able to fend off their attacks because of Cadar's fortification, but the moment we leave the protection of its walls, we're as good as dead. The stormbirds have hundreds of deathstalkers to contend with, so they cannot assist with the imbalanced ratio of our soldiers to Ashaat's."

Elize unclasped his hands and pulled away. Lines etched across her brow, tugged at the corners of her eyes. Silver hairs lined the crown of her head, fading into the fiery red hue once dominant, but no less beautiful. Where the body began its slow dance with death, one falling leaf at a time, one sunset after the other, the spirit livened with every moment, with every realization that time was a gift far more precious than wealth. It was something the humans fathomed best; a fleeting life one-fifth the length of a nyrian's but no less potent, no less meaningful. And Igtheos would die the day hers ended, one way or another.

"He can't have them," Elize's voice wavered, but determination set deep into her jade green eyes. "I will carry their locations to my pyre."

"You'd sacrifice our supporters' lives? Our daughter's?"

"I will sacrifice *everything* to stop the world from destroying itself, Igtheos. Even you."

"I know."

They held each other's gaze. The fire pot's radiance dwindled, leaving the room to wallow in the gray pallor of the moons.

When Igtheos could no longer stand the silence, he opened the bottle of wine he'd handpicked for their reunion, poured a glass, and offered it to Elize. She refused.

"There has to be a way to get the civilians out," Elize said as she unfastened her braid. "Cadar must have a passage used by city officials in times of crisis."

Igtheos downed the glass of wine before answering. "There is such a passage, but it doesn't matter. There's no way to sneak hundreds of people quietly out of a city at the same time, no matter what kind of distraction you create."

"Then we lie to him. Tell him we agree to his treaty."

"And then what? He'll keep you in irons, march you around Quinaria with a knife at your throat until you've revealed all the scrolls' locations, and probably keep Zaria hostage for collateral."

"Zaria." Elize practically growled their daughter's name, her body bristling as she tucked a loose curl behind her ear. "She'll be long gone, far from this cursed land with you and the rest of the rebellion. Take the stormbirds and find refuge in Orillon."

Igtheos snorted. "Orillon? They'd as soon welcome a death-stalker horde than shelter nyrians."

"Neharem, then."

"Even if we elicited compassion from one of the tribes, even if we found ships great enough to carry all those true to our cause to their sanctuary, and even if you convince Ashaat to take you and you alone while the rest of us go free..." Igtheos swallowed. He took Elize in his arms, traced a thumb over her cheek. "The death he'd give you would not be swift and painless."

"The best things in life demand no shortage of sacrifice."

Before he could conjure a rebuttal, she led him to the bed and climbed on top of him, any trace of anger in her eyes replaced with the heat of passion. She removed his outer robe and kissed his chest, trailing down to his stomach where she loosened the sash holding his tunic in place. He pulled it over his head and started to return the favor when the door creaked open.

"Papa?"

Igtheos hastened to throw a sheet over his exposed groin. A petite figure hesitated in the doorway, silhouetted by a sconce aglow in the hallway. The faintest whimper arose.

Elize smoothed her clothes and rose to meet their daughter. "Zaria, come here. It's late, my darling. What are you still doing up?"

Zaria's small feet pattered across the floor. She sat on the bed between them and grabbed at the excess fabric of her sleeping gown, twisting and kneading it into small pleats. Sunset orange locks streaked with white tumbled about her face. In the dim light of the room, one couldn't make out the unevenness of her skin tone, the subtle clashing of Elize's cream patches against his dominant golden hues—proof of their unholy union. A child that never should have been. Zaria was at the core of what the rebellion stood for, a slap in the face to old wives' tales and religious rumors, for she represented both humans and nyrians, dispelling the lies that either were superior, that either had more or less of a right to breathe, live, and love. So rare it was for a nyman to be conceived, much less born. She was Igtheos's most precious gift.

And his greatest weakness.

"I had a bad dream," Zaria whispered, curling her hand into his.

Igtheos tucked her hair behind her pointed ear. "Again?"

Elize shot him a look but didn't dare pry in the presence of their already distraught daughter.

"Mhmm." Zaria didn't look up. "But tonight was different. He was in my room. He..." She wiped a lone tear trailing down her cheek, then tucked her head into her knees.

That was enough for Elize. She wrapped their daughter in her cloak, casually covering part of the girl's head and muffling her ears in the process. "In her room?" she hissed to Igtheos. "What madness does she speak of?"

Igtheos traced the edge of his dagger's hilt and wrapped his fingers around its turquoise pommel. "They're a child's nightmares, Elize. Let it go."

"I will not. You've no idea what I've borne witness to on my journeys, cannot begin to fathom the beings I've crossed paths with."

Zaria's head shot up from her mother's lap. "Mama, don't leave. I don't want it to get you."

Elize gave Igtheos a final glare, then took her daughter's face in her hands. "I'm not leaving again, my darling. Nothing is going to get me."

"But he wants you."

"Who wants me?"

"The monster with the empty eyes. He's always eating, Mama, but always hungry. And you made him angry."

A chill seized Igtheos's spine. He rose from the bed and strode to the balcony as a shadow passed over him; Araynia, returning from hunting over Skyfall Sea. The presence of his stormbird brought him a sliver of comfort.

"I'm taking our daughter back to bed," Elize called out behind him.

Igtheos nodded. "I eagerly await your return. We've much to discuss."

"We have nothing left to discuss," Elize whispered. "She is our miracle. I'll die a thousand deaths so that others like her may yet have the chance to live."

Zaria locked her gaze on him, one emerald eye and one like his, light and iridescent as the sky at dawn.

"Of course, my love." Igtheos kissed them both on the cheek, then lifted Elize's chin with the utmost tenderness. "You speak as though you hold the world in your hands."

"We all do." She returned the kiss and, with a hand on their daughter's back, made for the hallway. "But I choose to take responsibility where others do not."

The door closed. A piece of Igtheos's heart left with them.

ELIZE

One hour. One hundred words.

According to Elize's calculations, her interaction with Ashaat wouldn't require more than that, and possibly—hopefully—less. Even if he drew it out, she wouldn't give him the courtesy of civility, not after what she'd been through, and most certainly not after what he'd done. He could playact all he liked. It didn't make him less of a cold-blooded murderer, of a dictator high on self and low on compassion, of a monster creeping through the shadows, leeching newborns from their mothers' breasts. And that wasn't even an exaggeration, sickening as it was.

Elize drew the hooded shawl back from her face. Clouds shielded the midday sun from her fair skin, and there was no point in trying to mask her identity, anyway. Ashaat's well-armed soldiers had tailed their small entourage from the moment they exchanged the security of the palace for the haunting cries of seahawks swarming above the peninsula's coastline. As they descended the final steps of the stone staircase leading from the city gates and trudged through the pink-tinted sand to the bridge of one of the many islands Ashaat and his sycophants had holed up in, Elize's pace slowed. How much of the man she knew remained behind those cool, scheming eyes? If she couldn't sway him, couldn't convince him of her sincerity, there'd be no hope for Igtheos's rebels, let alone their daughter.

One last confrontation. One last lie.

"I'm less than inclined to see the monstrous bastard myself, my lady, but it's best not to leave the negotiating to your husband, eh?" a gruff voice said behind her.

A grin tugged at the corners of Elize's lips. "Of course not, Halmand."

Igtheos's general, his right hand, scowled at one of Ashaat's soldiers who'd dared to strut too close to Elize. The clenching of his fists was enough to frighten the young soldier a safe distance back, and Elize tipped her chin in gratitude. Halmand was a surly human with broad shoulders and a far too neatly styled bun, given his time spent in battle, but his heart was one of the purest she'd ever known. He cleared his throat and bowed with an outstretched arm.

Elize dug her sandaled feet further into the sand, wishing, for the briefest of moments, that she'd never returned to her homeland. Ahead, trailing Igtheos, marched a handful of rebels armed with spears and sickle swords. They looked naked compared to Ashaat's soldiers lined up on either side of the bridge like statues, their weapons sharp, their armor untouched by battle. Where Igtheos's rebels were lucky to acquire enough leather or bronze to reinforce their tunics, Ashaat's men (for no women were allowed in his army, except to warm the soldiers' beds) were outfitted in lyvium, a newly discovered metal that had no match in lightness or integrity. From it, they'd fashioned helmets and cuirasses, and the occasional high-ranking soldier had forearm and shin guards to match—not to mention their weapons, fine short swords composed of steel, spears and javelins with lyvium heads, and shields that could actually hold their own against a barrage of attacks.

Gods. How had Igtheos survived as long as he did?

"No one will think less of you if you're not feeling up to the task..." Halmand's voice trickled away with his gaze, snapping Elize out of her stupor.

She forced her feet forward, chin high, with a proud set to her jaw. "I'm always up for a task, General, no matter how much it goes against my better judgment. It's a miracle I'm not dead yet."

Halmand nodded curtly, but Elize caught the twinkle in his amber eyes as she passed him and stepped onto the rickety planking of the bridge. Water lapped at its edges, teasing the worn, bleached wood. Ocean spray stung her face and filled her nostrils with its salty musk as she side-stepped around piles of bird excrement, her pace quickening until she fell into step behind two of Igtheos's warriors.

Nevethium sconces greeted them when they reached the island, their dark-green hues cold and foreboding in the fog's shroud. They adorned not only the large war tent Ashaat had constructed for his temporary palace, but also the makeshift courtyard that, based on the few remaining trampled stalks, had once been a kuba crop. Apparently, Ashaat no longer saw fit to use the islands surrounding Cadar proper for agriculture and fishing. Elize kneeled to retrieve a loose kuba grain and twisted it between her fingers. Such a small symbol of life, but no less powerful, no less meaningful. How appropriate its demise to be crushed beneath the sandals of one of Ashaat's soldiers. Little did they know what he sought to unleash upon an innocent, ignorant world.

The soldiers guarding the entrance to the tent crossed their spears as Igtheos approached. They wore spiked pauldrons and had wrapped their faces with dark, embroidered silks, leaving only their eyes exposed—a new style implemented by Ashaat to strip them of their individuality, she presumed. He'd always had a flair for the dramatic.

Igtheos's face was stone as he lowered one of the guard's spears with his bare hand. "No need for the show of arms. Your master expects me, and I'm well aware you have my party outnumbered a hundred to one."

A cruel laugh erupted from inside the tent.

The other guard cast a hesitant glance behind himself, then lowered his spear as well. "Your men will remain outside."

"Of course. All but my general and my advisor."

The guard glared at Elize, taking in the shortness of her ears, the redness of her braided hair, but he stepped aside.

Igtheos ducked beneath the divided canvas and disappeared into the tent. Elize waited as long as possible, until the guards' gazes intensified and Halmand shifted uneasily behind her, and then, clenching the crescent moon-shaped brooch that fastened her cloak, she stepped inside.

Silence swallowed Elize as she entered, the room so still, its inhabitants so attuned, she had no choice but to endure the heated stares of a dozen enemies boring into her like the sun's unhindered rays. She kept her own eyes down, but she could still feel them watching, tracking, judging as she took her place beside Igtheos. A woolen rug lay beneath her feet, patterned in threes. Three colors, three lines, three diamonds. Reminiscent of the moons, and the Vysilliam, the original and worthiest trinity of races, lest any lowly human forget their place. Fists clenched, Elize raised her head to face the monster in his makeshift throne.

A monster he was. There was no one as cunning; no one as beautiful. That was what made someone monstrous, after all. The evil beneath the beauty, beneath the allure, beneath the magnificence. For who would approach a monster otherwise?

Ashaat sat regally in his sun-blood wood throne, its crimson hue complimenting the ruby pin that held his nyrian white locks in place atop his head. He wore polished lyvium armor from neck to toe, layered atop an embroidered tunic. A knife dangled from his left hand. He twisted it about, lifted it to his face to inspect it, and twisted it some more, all while staring idly about the room as though the circumstances couldn't be more irritating. To Ashaat's left, shrouded in darkness, stood his advisor, Kalmech. The nyrian's white hair was pulled back in a thin braid, accenting his pointed ears and sharp nose. He held a large bound book, likely filled with whatever dark sorcery Ashaat had dabbled in as of late, and he drew it closer to his chest when he noticed Elize's gaze lingering on him.

Igtheos cleared his throat, and then, and only then, did Ashaat toss a glance in their direction, his golden eyes well masking the internal monologue of his mind.

Ashaat raised a silver-blue hand, his chin tipped with that defiance he never seemed to be able to shake, even when no one dared to defy him. "Be at ease, my friends. They've come at my call, and there's no need to fear a sandcat who's been declawed and defanged."

A few chuckles arose from the nyrians lucky enough to find places in Ashaat's would-be court, though the room felt no more at ease than it had moments prior. Heat overtook Elize's cheeks, not out of discomfort or embarrassment, but out of the unshake-able sense that she didn't belong in the tent, on the island, in a nation so full of hatred and prejudice, no matter the fact that she'd been born there just like the rest of them, that she'd tended the land and sought betterment for all.

"It's been too long, old friend. There was once a time not so long ago when an outsider could scarcely tell where I ended and you began."

Elize didn't need to look up to know Ashaat addressed her. It was partially a slight to Igtheos, ignoring him and his war general, but also not entirely a lie. Though, if they were ever truly friends, it wasn't in the conventional sense. Ashaat collected friends like one might collect knives, seeking the sharpest or most beautiful, at least until a better version came along. Elize had long since been replaced.

"You leave such a lasting impression that I could go a thousand lifetimes without you and still feel as though we'd shared company only the day prior," she replied.

Igtheos raised an eyebrow, a quick, subtle gesture. Elize skirted her gaze away from his. She hated herself a bit for falling back into banter with Ashaat despite all that had transpired, but it was so easily done with him. He drew it from people with finely tuned skill, like a spider seducing its prey. She was no exception. But she was smart, smarter than most and well enough attuned to his ways to at least recognize it happening. Awareness was everything.

Ashaat flashed a row of spotless teeth and traced the knife's tip across his bottom lip. "Igtheos," he said, nodding to her husband. He sneered at Halmand. "Igtheos's bitch." The general's face turned red enough to rival sun-blood blossoms, but he managed to keep his tongue in check. Unsatisfied with the lack of rise, Ashaat leaned back in his chair with a leg swung over the armrest. "You're all here, so I imagine you've found my proposition agreeable?"

Igtheos crossed his arms. "Anything seems agreeable when your people are on the brink of starvation, but you already know that."

"I knew an honorable, selfless leader like you couldn't sacrifice innocents, no matter how little their worth." Ashaat shrugged, his expression one of disinterest. "Now, about the scrolls."

Elize was acutely aware of the onlookers' gazes still boring into her back and did her best to pretend they didn't exist. "I don't have them here."

Another grin pulled at the corner of Ashaat's mouth. "I'd be rather disappointed if you did." He kept fiddling with the knife, but Elize knew she had his undivided attention.

"They're spread all over Quinaria," she continued, fighting the quaver in her voice. "It took me ages to hide them."

"And it will take a moon cycle or two at most to acquire them. Half that time was spent on one of your obscure pilgrimages, and I'll be sending dozens of men after them as opposed to vulnerable, little you navigating the wild alone."

Elize resisted the urge to defend herself by detailing the trials she'd overcome to get the scrolls safely hidden, and she didn't dare mention what terrors awaited him should he locate a single one. No need to snuff out his confidence.

She crossed her arms tightly against her stomach. "So, we have an accord?"

Kalmech's face curdled. He came to stand directly beside the throne, spindly fingers still clutching the book. "My lord, there's the matter of her honesty. If she leads us astray with even one of the scroll's locations, we may find ourselves on a never-ending ghost hunt at best, and with countless lives lost at worst."

"This is why I love having you on my council," Ashaat said with a sardonic sort of amusement. "Endless optimism."

"He has a point, husband."

A waif of a figure emerged from the screen behind Ashaat's throne. She wore a dress made from a black material woven so thinly one could make out every curve of her body. The same silken hair as Ashaat's cascaded past her shoulders, accentuating the same silver-blue skin, framing the same piercing eyes. They weren't siblings, for he had none as far as Elize knew, but she had to be a cousin or some other relative close enough in blood but not too close. Apparently, Ashaat had taken his nyrian pure-blood complex up a notch.

The woman had a look of general disdain, but when her gaze flickered over Elize, the pout of her full lips stretched into a frown, and the faintest hint of a wrinkle creased in her otherwise flawless forehead.

Elize held the woman's gaze, much to her own discomfort.

"Ryiana, I fear you haven't met my old... friends." Ashaat practically laughed the last word, as though it had been such a humorous term a few minutes ago that it deserved another go around.

"Your enemy, your enemy's right hand, and... " Ryiana pursed her lips, studying, contemplating, eyes cool. Her gaze hadn't left Elize. "The traitor."

It took all Elize's resolve to bite back the comments bubbling in her throat. Traitor? She was the only one loyal to the Prophets' Creed, so loyal she stashed away the knowledge to save the world from Ashaat and the prophets who'd strayed into darkness with him. To save them from themselves.

But there was no point in bemoaning her position now, all the wrongs they'd committed, all her rights. Those who could be won already had been.

"I assume you'll want some form of leverage to ensure my cooperation and honesty," Elize said to Ashaat. She took some pride in the fact that she'd snubbed his cousin-wife outright instead of engaging in frivolous jabs. "I'm willing to comply, as long as you know my daughter is not to be involved in our negotiations."

Igtheos stirred beside her. Her hand ached to reach out and take his, but she refused to show any vulnerability in front of their enemies.

The devilish grin hadn't left Ashaat's lips. "I wouldn't dream of it." He rose, gave Ryiana a pat on the shoulder that visibly ruffled her, and came to stand directly in front of Elize. "Though I have no children of my own, I know how precious they will be one day. Especially given the miraculous abomination yours is. I hear she's not even all that hideous. Ten fingers, ten toes, and only mild disfigurement."

"We want rations sent over within a week's time," Igtheos said, a little too loudly, the heat in his voice just a touch below raging. "Freedom to come and go as we please from Cadar proper. No harassment from your soldiers. No threats. A complete armistice until an appointed date. Call off your bugs, and I'll do the same with our stormbirds."

"Done." Ashaat wiped his hands against each other as if cleansing some unseen dirt, then offered one to Igtheos.

Elize contained her surprise. Halmand didn't. A gasp escaped his throat, and he made a rather conspicuous face at her that screamed mistrust.

Igtheos extended a cautious hand. "You've no counteroffer?"

Ashaat shrugged, shook Igtheos's hand as though it pained him, then wiped his hands once again as he retreated to his throne. "I expected no less, and even a little more. We're both aware of the impasse we've reached, and I don't know about you, but I'm quite tired of playing at war."

Playing at war. The way he so casually regarded the thousands of lives already lost made Elize's stomach swim. But of course he didn't care, not when there was a far greater prize.

"Besides," Ashaat continued, "I'll soon have a far greater prize."

Elize winced.

"And Cadar?" Igtheos asked, the same way a child might press their parents to stay up just a bit later.

"She's yours. For now. We can carve her up once Elize is done with her part of the bargain." Ashaat retrieved his knife from the armrest and resumed running his fingertips across the flat side of the blade. "There are a great deal of details to work out, but as long as we are all in agreement, I'm happy to conclude this meeting."

Elize didn't wait to see if Igtheos would accept. "I want something in writing. Tonight. Before our witnesses and yours."

She didn't know what schemes he'd concocted, if any, but everything seemed to be going a little too smoothly. Ashaat wasn't one to make vague agreements. He preferred everything laid out before him like a war general's map table, all options on display, all potential threats listed and addressed. This recklessness was either a sign of his unraveling, or theirs.

Ashaat wedged the tip of the blade into the armrest. "I'd planned to have a rather lengthy agreement prepared for tomorrow now that we have an accord, but if it eases your storm, Kalmech can draw up a preliminary version right now."

"It would." Elize watched closely as a disgruntled Kalmech retrieved some parchment and a quill from behind the screen.

"And, as proof of my goodwill and benevolent nature, I'll see to it my soldiers bring in a feast for you and yours this very evening. Allow us passage through a gate of your choosing, and I'll send in an unarmed batch of grunts with all the wine, kuba grain, and wild boar you can eat." Ashaat's gaze locked onto Elize's, and for a moment, there was no one else in the room. "I may even throw in some sedare mushrooms, for old time's sake."

Elize only nodded. No words would come out.

As the rest of the tent blurred around her and people scurried about making preparations, Elize withdrew into herself. She found a cushion in the corner. Sat.

Something felt off, like the silence of the woods before a forest fire. But she couldn't pin down what it was, or even prove that her intuition was anything more than an awareness of how obviously eager Ashaat was to get his grasping fingers on the scrolls. He'd do and say anything to get them, just as she'd do and say anything to give their rebellion a fighting chance.

They'd have to wait and see whose bluff held out.

IGTHEOS

The scent of roasted boar permeated the feasting hall, the skin of one crackling and crisping on a spit as its dripping fat teased the flames below. Forgotten songs rose above the laughter and chatter, filling the room with melodies so long absent it almost seemed eerie, as though the songs belong to a different time, to warriors who'd earned their victory instead of hiding under the guise of a ruse. And the smoke, formally a sign of impending defeat, now signified ceremony and good tidings.

A gift, part of him hoped. *A curse,* argued another.

No matter what lay ahead, Igtheos had no choice but to be grateful for the festivities as they unfolded around him in the form of dancing lovers tossing their heads back in wine-infused stupors. Or there, in the bellies of his soldiers, finally filled with much deserved food and drink after getting by on rations scarcely fit for a child. And though he questioned the morality of his own euphoria, the ease of his muscles, the lack of tension in his jaw, part of him knew deep down that he deserved it. The entire rebellion did. All throughout the room—and likely all throughout the city—everyone laughed, dozed, feasted, and danced, their faces alight with the widest of grins or relaxed in the deepest of slumbers.

All but Elize. She sat straight, her gaze locked on the flames in the way one might regard a funeral pyre. Occasionally, her attention flicked to Zaria, to him, and she'd force a quick grin for their sake only to quickly retreat into her macabre shell, looming like a stone guardian over the room. She'd said little since leaving the island that afternoon, but she didn't have to. Igtheos was no fool. He knew as well as she that Ashaat wasn't to be trusted. Of course, the elitist devil played at something, plotted even as he offered them gifts and promises of peace. But they'd known that going in. The whole point was to abate his hunger by offering him the illusion of their ignorance while they worked to outsmart him, to escape, to give their people a fighting chance.

He had no cause to question their plan's effectiveness.

"For a man with a belly full of wine and eternal gratitude from his thousands of followers, you've got quite the downtrodden mouth," Halmand said, knocking his golden chalice into Igtheos's.

"I've intertwined my life with another's, and when she's having a less than splendid time, I find myself in a similar disposition." Igtheos took a tentative sip and rolled his eyes in Elize's direction.

"My lad does that to me as well. Hence my celebratory mood."

Igtheos searched the room until he found Halmand's son, Dom, a boy of seven-and-ten, dark curls plastered to his flushed face as he tried his hand with a soldier ten years his senior. The woman was not having it, and, to the boy's credit, he bowed clumsily and took another swig before approaching a girl more suited to his station.

"I see. Did he inspire you to loot gold from the storerooms as well?" Igtheos's tone was one of mild irritation, but he knew Halmand could read through his sarcasm, no matter how convincing of a show he put on. "I'm sure I don't need to remind you we aren't here for their riches, nor will it resolve any of our problems at present. That includes the chalices you tucked into your bedroll."

"Eh, just have Ass-hat write it into the treaty."

With that, Halmand downed the rest of his drink and poured a refill until it dripped over the sides. Elize snickered briefly before regaining her composure, and for that, Igtheos could've kissed Halmand. Before he could thank him, Dom ran up to where Igtheos, Elize, Halmand, and the other generals sat at the head of the room, amid the remnants of supply crates stacked around them like a makeshift fortress.

"Father, your lyvium dagger," Dom panted, his eyes dreamy with drink. "May I see it? Arianna doesn't believe our family was part of the blacksmith's guild, being human and all."

"Who the fuck is Arianna?" Halmand narrowed his eyes as he rose to survey the room. "Take me to her, and I'll set the record straight."

Dom appeared to sober in an instant. "Er... that won't be necessary. I actually need to take a piss, so I'm just going to step outside for a—"

"That dark-haired beauty?" Halmand bellowed. He took another swig and slapped Dom's back. "Good taste, lad, good taste. I'll make sure you don't make a fool of yourself."

With that, the father marched toward the unsuspecting woman seated a few tables away, his reluctant son lagging and muttering unintelligible protests under his breath.

Igtheos nudged Elize, hoping to rouse a response from her, some shared humor of what their future as parents might look like, but she only offered a ghost of a smile, the kind that suggested she hadn't paid attention to the situation, hadn't absorbed a word they'd exchanged.

"You might allow yourself to dabble in some merriment, just this once," he muttered, half expecting her not to hear it.

Elize's eyes narrowed. She turned to face him like a stormbird locking onto its prey. "Unlike you, I won't partake in ill-timed revelry."

Igtheos endeavored to let the comment hang in the air until the tension fizzled out between them, but he was already three glasses of wine in.

"You had equal voice in our meeting," he said, grinding the base of his chalice against the table's edge. "If you had concerns, why did you not contest them? Why accept his gifts? We all signed the treaty. I don't recall you objecting."

"Because my people are starving." Elize drew her cloak tighter about her shoulders; not that she needed to be wearing it in the first place. The room was warmer than a bathhouse during the Feasting Moons.

"Your people? Really, Elize? *I'm* the one who's fought beside them these two years, not you."

Elize averted her gaze, but Igtheos knew he'd gone too far the moment the words left his lips.

He came to stand beside her, rubbed her shoulders. "Forgive me. We both knew you had to go, and that it could only be you. I care about what happens to the humans, and so do many nyrians loyal to me. What Ashaat wants is an unjust world, more so than it already is, and *our* people will not stand idly by and let that happen. We are the true Nyzarians, the true followers of Chai'Tik."

Thin, pale fingers covered his own golden ones. She didn't turn to face him, but the warmth of her hand signaled a truce between them. Perhaps even a peace offering.

Halmand returned from interrogating his son's newest love interest, and, upon noting Igtheos's disposition, slid silently onto the bench that ran the length of the table, selecting a spot not too close, but still close enough to eavesdrop.

Bastard.

Igtheos didn't give him the satisfaction. He brought the chalice to his lips and tried to revert his outlook to the one he'd held minutes prior, but it danced further out of reach, separated by the chasm of reality. All around them, more and more people dozed off, relishing bliss, some snuggled together, most with a drink in hand. A musician plucked a soft medley to himself, a lullaby Igtheos recognized from childhood.

In a world of endless night,
Where hope has vanished out of sight,
The shadows deepen, the moons are gone,
And all seems lost, and forever undone.

Here the winds are harsh and cold,
And the world is cruel, good stories untold,
The rivers flow with a mournful dirge,
And the skies above, with darkness merge.

In this realm of endless despair,
Where nothing is fair, and love is rare,
The hearts of all are filled with pain,
And souls are shattered, while loved ones are slain.

But in the darkness, a spark ignites,
A glimmer of hope, amidst the endless night,
For though the world may fall and fade,
A new life awaits, in an eternal glade.

"He knows he can free that monster with the scrolls," Elize whispered when the song ended, her hand clutching his own.

"Ashaat will never touch them again, I swear it to you. We'll lead him on a ghost hunt, like you said. We will... *I* will..." Igtheos silenced the roars of pride echoing in his heart. "I'll seek refuge in Neharem."

Elize looked over her shoulder at him, her green eyes wide.

"You said yourself Chai'Tik has taken up residence there," Igtheos continued, keenly aware of Halmand still eavesdropping. He reclaimed his spot on the bench to make it clear he wasn't hiding anything, that if he didn't want Halmand to be privy to their conversation, he wouldn't be. "If a goddess found them amicable, why shouldn't we? Their land is well-stewarded, and humans and nyrians have coexisted peacefully for years within certain tribes. Some may even welcome nymans."

He followed Elize's gaze to where Zaria slept, still seated at a table, her face happily nestled in a pile of cooled kuba grain.

"I mean, you'd trade our civil unrest for warring tribes and less than ideal living situations," Halmand butted in. "But sure, no Ass-hat, so they've already won me over. Assuming they don't kill us on sight."

His candor prompted a genuine smile from Elize. "You could try being civil for once," she said in the way she might chide Zaria. "It's surprising how far a little decency takes you."

Halmand offered a snort of a laugh in response, wine spilling down his beard and onto his exposed chest where his tunic cut low as he drained the chalice. For a human, he could hold his drink well, but even he had pushed the limits of his merry-making tonight. Elize looked on with amusement, though her fingers continued to tap at the stone table, pick at the meat, swirl the wine around in her cup, all without consuming, without enjoying.

A chill seized Igtheos's spine. He wouldn't call Elize a seer, but she had a knack for reading people and situations with impec-

cable scrutiny. She'd prophesied many unions—theirs includ-
ed. Knew the sex of their unborn child, predicted the droughts,
the law changes, the exploitation. Foresaw the downfall of the
Nyzarian republic.

She was one of the Prophets, after all. Perhaps one of the
finest ever, sprouted from the lineage of the only humans ever
to lay a finger on the scrolls of the gods, to be considered worthy
enough to put one to ink herself.

And trusted by the gods to destroy them.

Or hide them. Igtheos assumed she had a good reason for
changing their plan at the last moment, without consulting him
or the other rebel leaders.

"I think I'll retire," Elize said, touching his shoulder.

Before Igtheos could object, Dom clinked a bottle of wine with
his cup to draw attention, doing so a little too forcefully. The
bottle cracked and sent dark, purple liquid cascading over the
sides and pooling onto the table. It stained the tunic of the rebel
nearest him, but the man was too drunk to notice—or care.
Dom cleared his throat and climbed up on the table, cup raised
high and head down as though he had to mentally prepare
himself for the wisdom he was about to bestow upon the room.
Beside Igtheos, Halmand grumbled, but his eyes gleamed with
pride.

"Attention-seeking little mutt, isn't he?" the general mur-
mured.

"Undeniably so," Igtheos said. "I wonder where he gets it."

Before Halmand could reply, Dom's borderline pubescent
voice flooded the great hall with a steadiness beyond his years.

"To our fearless leader," the boy began. "For guiding our arrows, stoking our courage, and shepherding us to this moment
of victory when we worried our little rebellion never stood a
chance. You showed us there were other nyrians like you who

understood equality. We aren't the height of our ears or the color of our hair or the days of our beating hearts, are we?"

That roused a cheer from the humans in the crowd while the handful of nyrians nodded in approval.

"No, we're much, much more." The boy was enamored by his own zeal now, pacing the table, his eyes wide, his arms fanned out as though he strove to rally more shouts of agreement. "The gods created us too, so how could anyone deem us less than worthy? Igtheos knows that. He cares. He leads. He loves." Dom locked eyes with Igtheos. The passion was so deep, so evident, that Igtheos couldn't help but return it. "I love my father, sir, but if the gods willed me to be sired by any other, it would only be you."

Igtheos stole a glance at Halmand. No jealousy stained his face. He simply basked in the boldness of his son with an adoration known only by a parent.

Dom strode to the end of the table, barely dodging hands and platters, and raised his glass to Igtheos. "To you, our selfless leader. When I have a son one day"—he paused to wink at a few of the adjacent women, most of whom rolled their eyes—"I will name him after you, and I will tell him how you fought for our freedom. And won."

Igtheos raised his cup in return. Drank with all the sincerity he could muster while people shouted and clapped in the background. No one outside of the attendees of the meeting knew the conditions of their bountiful meal. If informed, Dom might rethink his claim, decide neither him nor his father a suitable choice for a namesake. Great leaders didn't begrudgingly accept their enemy's terms out of desperation, or risk the lives of their people in a less-than-guaranteed escape plan when most of them would've been much happier fighting to the death.

But he was the one left to make those difficult decisions, and make them he would. Whatever saved them. Whatever gave Elize the time she needed. She was the real savior.

Igtheos looked to her for comfort; found her seat abandoned. She likely stole away during the toast. He glanced at the chair where Zaria had slept. Also empty.

He rose to search for them, but Halmand clapped a meaty hand on his shoulder.

"Did you hear my lad?" the general sputtered. His eyes glistened as he pulled Igtheos closer. "The respect he has for you? The love? You stop doubting yourself and your decision, alright? You've inspired a generation of folks that will never forget this. Their children's children's children's children... " Halmand looked up at the ceiling as if he were trying to calculate exactly how long this inspiration would last. "People way down the fucking line, Igtheos, they'll remember this rebellion and what it meant to the visionary nation of Quinaria. So don't you forget it. You and that beautiful wife and child of yours, you don't forget it."

Halmand yanked him in for a bone-crushing hug. Igtheos silenced the nagging voices for a moment. Returned the hug. He *had* made the right decision, and with Elize's aid, they would see this through, bring forth a new world, one the gods would be proud to reside in again.

He had no choice but to believe.

ELIZE

*S*moke.

Elize shot up in bed and blinked rapidly until her eyes adjusted to the darkness. The fire bowls in the bedchamber weren't lit, but smoke hung thick in the air, clinging to the hairs in her nostrils and filling her lungs. She flung out her arm to feel for her loved ones. Zaria snored blissfully against her, but Igtheos's spot beyond their daughter was cold.

"Zaria, wake up." Elize tried to mask the panic gripping her voice as she shook her daughter's shoulders.

The girl muttered something and rolled over.

Elize ripped the blanket off and yanked her up. A scream echoed from somewhere outside, and her heart raced in response. Zaria started to whine. Elize clamped her hand over her daughter's mouth.

"Listen, and listen well, my moonlight." Elize waited for Zaria to give a wary but compliant nod, then took the girl's face in her hands. "Something's wrong. I don't want you to worry, but I do need you to be on guard. If I tell you to hush, you hush. If I tell you to run, you run. If I tell you to hide, you disappear and only come out for someone you trust. Do you understand?"

Zaria's lips trembled. "Where's Papa?"

"We'll find him. Tell me you understand."

Another scream rattled the night.

"I understand," Zaria whispered.

"Good." Elize grabbed her daughter's cloak and sandals from the bedside. "Put these on. Quickly."

While Zaria complied, albeit at a slower pace than Elize's racing heart would've liked, she threw on her own traveling clothes: a leather tunic, leggings of the same make, and a woolen cloak large enough to mask her from head to toe. Pulling on her boots, she hobbled to the balcony and thrust the curtains out of the way.

A small gasp caught in Elize's throat. The glow of flames illuminated the night sky, casting an eerie orange hue over the city. Screams and cries filled the air, dimmed by the roar of the inferno. The sound of crackling fire and shattering glass echoed through the streets below as buildings collapsed beneath flames that danced and flickered. And the smoke... its acrid scent drew tears from her eyes.

Chai'Tik save us.

Elize stumbled away from the balcony. A spear leaned against a wooden chest in the corner of the room; one of Igtheos's many spare weapons. She tightened her fingers around the shaft. It was heavier than she expected, its weight unbalanced and dangerous in her slender fingers, its point gleaming in the moonlight.

Elize tiptoed past her daughter and pressed her hand to the door. Hot as cast-iron pan over open flames. She considered calling for help or shouting a warning to others who slept in adjacent rooms, but whomever started the fires was already within their walls. Waiting. Watching.

"Come, my moonlight."

Elize grabbed Zaria's arm and led her across the room to where a tapestry showcasing the trinity of the three original Vysilliam races hung the length of the wall. The shaktar, hovering above the nyrian and myrem, glared down on her from its

thread perch, its leathery wings spread, striking a more beautiful—yet no less villainous—pose than the actual creatures
she'd encountered not two moon cycles past. She glared back as
though the fabric might convey her contempt to the actual beings
it represented, then drew the tapestry aside, tracing her fingertips along the indentations of the stone wall until she found the
trigger Igtheos had shown her. It gave beneath her fingertips,
groaning, announcing their location to any who lingered nearby,
and she and Zaria disappeared into the cool, darkened tunnels
of the hidden passageway.

They relied on Elize's nevethium pendant to guide their way
through the shadows, pausing every so often to listen. Elize's
boot landed on something prickly, something alive, and a chill
crawled up her spine as it skittered away, hissing. She raised
her pendant higher and caught sight of a long, thin tail ending
in a tuft of bristly hair as it slipped around the corner.

Zaria's nails dug into her palm. "Mama, are there skirvin in
here?"

Elize managed a dry swallow. Of course the damn rodents
were in here, their razor-sharp spines sticking out in all di-
rections from their pale, sickly gray skin. They made their
home underground, in tunnels, in crypts and dungeons and cel-
lars, seeking prey with their impeccable hearing and sensitive
whiskers, spikes poised to poison any predator who drew too
near.

"Of course not, darling." Elize squeezed Zaria's hand and
tugged her forward. "Hurry, please."

The further they ventured, the louder and more frequent the
screams grew, and Elize all but forgot the fiendish creatures
lurking in the passage. Her heart leaped with each thud, each
cry, each clash of metal, and though Zaria gripped her hand as

if the girl knew her life depended on it, she kept as quiet as the mist.

When they reached what appeared to be a dead end, Elize hovered her crystal near the wall until she found a slightly discolored stone. She gave a last glance at Zaria and, trusting her daughter to heed her earlier warning, pressed her weight into the stone.

The grinding wall roared like thunder. Elize held the spear in what she hoped was a fighting stance as a room appeared before them. The darkness was only a faint shadow compared to the passageway, and the aroma of roasted boar and sweet spices filled the air.

The feasting hall.

Elize's eyes detected no visible movement in the great room spread before her, but she tucked her pendant away all the same as she inched away from the shelter of the tunnel, spear first. The rebels were strewn about tables and cushions as she'd left them earlier that evening, but someone should've stirred, been alerted by the secret passage opening.

An icy wave of fear washed over Elize's heart. Part of her wanted to disappear back into the passage, but another part knew she couldn't live with the guilt if her people were simply passed out from drinking and she left them there, vulnerable, while danger lurked nearby.

"Stay here," she whispered to Zaria.

Elize crept into the hall. The nearest rebel lay well over twenty feet away, so she stopped every few paces to glance back at Zaria, to ensure the girl remained in the secret passage. Her breathing hitched when she reached the rebel, a young woman sprawled on the floor with long, dark hair fanned behind her like a fish-tail. A silent prayer danced on Elize's lips as she grabbed the woman's shoulder and rolled her over.

Zaria gasped.

A wave of nausea swept over Elize as her daughter's footsteps pattered over. She covered her Zaria's eyes; fought the urge to close her own. She forced her gaze back to the blood trickling from the gaping wound in the rebel's neck and pooling on the floor beneath her. Something had torn the tissue away, leaving serrated strips of flesh and a blood-soaked cavity in its stead.

Skulmor.

A tremble seized Elize's hands. They had no business in Nyzarian affairs, even during peacetime. Their violent presence could only mean one thing: they'd been made an offer they couldn't refuse. And the rebels had proposed no such exchange.

Zaria whimpered beside her.

Something moved at the edge of Elize's vision, and she glanced up from the body.

A scream caught in her throat.

Shadows danced at the far end of the hall. Not a trick of the eye or some imagined monster from Zaria's dreams. A living, breathing threat.

"When I say so, we run immediately back into the passageway," Elize whispered, quietly enough that not even a beridian could hear her.

But the creature across the room did. Two eyes appeared in the darkness, catching the dying embers of the fire bowls. One yellow, and one milky white. The skulmor emitted a low growl as the bulk of its form came into the light.

Elize had heard rumors of the wolven race's ferocity, knew Ashaat liked to capture and pit them against each other for a sick form of entertainment, but she'd never beheld the intensity of one up close. It was far larger than the tallest of nyrians, yet it moved on all fours like a common beast. It wore something akin to a loincloth around its nether regions, its fur presumably offering enough warmth otherwise. Pointed ears flicked forward. It prowled closer as its lips pulled back in a snarl, revealing two rows of sharp, yellowed fangs.

The perfect hunter.

Elize tightened her grip on Zaria's wrist. "Now."

Together, mother and daughter sprinted back toward the safety of the tunnel, their footsteps slapping across the stone floor. Elize dared to hope. Despite the skulmor's warrior physique, they were far closer to their means of escape than it was to them.

Sanctuary lay just feet away when a hulking figure leaped in front of them, cutting off their escape. Another skulmor. It lunged at them, jaws snapping. A scream scraped Elize's throat. She grabbed Zaria's sleeping gown and yanked her back just before its fangs snagged her.

Run. Hide.

Elize's instincts nearly overwhelmed her. But one screamed louder than the rest.

Protect.

"Stay behind me," Elize said, her own voice a growl, a warning. Keep away from her child, or she'd strike with everything she had.

The skulmor accepted the challenge. Raised its hackles as it circled them. In the corner of her eye, Elize caught the other skulmor creeping from across the room, as though it waited to see what its companion would do.

The one nearest attacked without warning, leaping into the air with its claws extended and a yawning jaw.

Elize angled the spearhead at its chest. The skulmor slammed into her, knocking her against Zaria and pinning them both to the ground. Matted fur smothered Elize's face. Her nostrils filled with the metallic stench of blood, the decay of rot. She waited for the pain, for the darkness.

It never came.

Groaning, Elize tried to shove the beast off her, but it was double her weight, maybe more. Zaria had stopped struggling beneath her.

Blood rushed in Elize's ears as she wriggled out from the skulmor. Her hands couldn't work fast enough as she gripped Zaria's forearms and pulled her into the cool of the room. The girl's two-toned eyes were closed, her mouth open. Elize swallowed a cry and pressed an ear to her chest.

A slow, steady beat thudded beneath.

Elize thanked Chai'Tik for her protection and crouched over her daughter like a sandcat. The feasting hall seemed to dance in the light from the fire pots as three more pairs of eyes emerged from beneath tables and what she now recognized as mounds of corpses. The skulmor she'd first noticed lurking was now close enough for her to make out the blood crusted around its mouth. She grabbed the spear still lodged in the dead one's chest and pulled. It didn't give at her first attempt, or the next. It only came free when she shouted, and she swore she heard ribs cracking as the winged spearhead made its exit. Blood dripped down the shaft as she raised the spear.

She could throw it at the encroaching skulmor. Run. But she might not be so lucky this time. There was no guarantee her spear would find its mark, or that she'd outrun the other three while carrying Zaria.

Elize glanced at the false wall. It gaped open, promising safety within its dark corridors. If she moved quickly, she might be able to throw Zaria inside, fend them off while the door closed, and pray to all the gods and goddesses in existence that the skulmor wouldn't find the pressure point to open the passage again.

She had to try.

Elize kneeled, spear in hand, and scooped up Zaria in one arm, remembering how light she'd once been, how her heart broke and remade itself in an instant the first time she laid eyes on the small squirming body still wet from the womb. She hadn't been the most available mother, had surely failed in some ways, but tonight, she'd make it up to Zaria. Tonight, she'd give her life again, no matter the cost.

A storm of energy swirled within Elize, her every step powerful as she hurtled toward the passageway. The skulmor were on her trail in an instant, eager to pursue their newfound prey.

I am no prey.

Elize's lungs rasped for air as she crossed the threshold of the passage, laid Zaria down like a limp doll, and slammed her hand so hard against the activation stone that it went numb. The false wall groaned closed painfully slow. A growl snapped her attention back to the hall where the skulmor ran at full speed.

The passage wasn't going to close in time. Elize brushed the hair off Zaria's forehead and planted a final, lingering kiss.

Spear lowered, she ran to meet her doom.

The false wall locked into place as she drove her spear into the skulmor who would've just narrowly slipped inside, giving Zaria a fighting chance. Igtheos was still alive somewhere in this tomb; she sensed it. Father and daughter would find one another, find safety, find triumph.

And the secret would die with her. The scrolls were forever out of Ashaat's reach. Until, perhaps, the right person came along, someone the scrolls would reveal themselves to, allowing things to be made right.

Elize clung to that belief as a chunk of flesh was torn from her leg, leaving a searing heat in its place. She gave a warrior's cry and flung herself at the skulmor.

Death was not the end.

IGTHEOS

"On your left!" Halmand shouted as he brought his blade down in a swift arc over a skulmor's neck.

Igtheos swung toward Halmand's claim, catching another skulmor's underbelly as it leaped for his throat. His sword ripped open its flesh, unleashing a torrent of blood and a slew of slimy organs that spilled and splattered onto the once pristine woolen rug, painting it a macabre shade of red. Igtheos's breath rasped against his throat. The great wolven warriors were unlike any enemies he'd fought in his two-hundred years, but any creature could be killed. Even the gods.

He swept his gaze over the room to ensure no adversaries remained. The small chamber, once used for scribing—given the rolls of parchment and shelf upon shelf of jars that likely stored ink—was doused in blood and littered with skulmor and rebel bodies. It was one of the last rooms they had searched on the main floor, and still no sign of Elize and Zaria.

Halmand ripped his short sword out of a skulmor carcass and hastily wiped it on his tunic. "We need to clear this gods-forsaken death trap, Igtheos. Every room has more of them than the rest, and the fire's all but sealed off the upper floors. If Elize..."

"She escaped." Igtheos closed the eyes of a rebel, a young man no more than twenty with a mop of hair as red as Elize's.

"I'm sure she did." Halmand wiped away a stray tear and stormed past him.

Igtheos let him go. A few words of sympathy danced on the tip of his tongue, but offering them now seemed crude. There was no time for comfort. Only justice.

He raced down the corridor after Halmand, his gaze searching every doorway, every dark corner, hoping his wife and child would appear instead of another monster. Elize was a light sleeper. He'd shown her the secret passage, and she was smart enough to navigate it. She would've awoken as soon as she heard a noise or smelled the smoke. She wasn't two wine glasses past gone like he'd been, sprawled out on the floor beside his soldiers, cup in hand. He usually held his wine well, though, even when indulging. And Halmand... the man was a legend. For him to fall asleep, too—nearly all their soldiers—someone had tampered with the food or drink they'd been gifted. Maybe both. A cold realization coiled around Igtheos's chest. Ashaat never intended to make peace, not even when it was to his advantage. Igtheos had assumed his upper hand with the snake and trusted him to play along.

And now he'd been bit.

Halmand appeared in the doorway of the room Igtheos had stalled in. "We need to give up this search. There's no telling what waste they've lain to the city or how many enemies lurk without the palace walls. If we don't leave now, this will become our tomb as well."

Igtheos didn't tell Halmand that he'd gladly accept the same fate as his loved ones, were it so. But part of him still believed they'd escaped, and if they had, they would've made their way out of the palace by now. He squeezed Halmand's forearm before easing into a jog down the hallway.

"Can we stop by the feasting hall again on our way out?" Halmand called after him. "Dom has... had our family crest, and I..." His voice broke. He furiously rubbed his eyes as though he didn't intend to let a single tear fall.

"Whatever you need." Tears threatened to well up in Igtheos's own eyes as he proceeded down the hallway. He didn't let them.

He'd scarcely had time to process what happened yet; he'd been awake less than an hour, but it felt like a lifetime. It wasn't the sound of screams or the shouts of pain that brought him to, but the sound of flesh ripping apart. He'd pushed his groggy body upright and found a pack of skulmor descending on his mostly unconscious soldiers, ripping through them like foxes set upon sleeping, grounded fowl. The floor was slick with blood. A blinding rage had overtaken him as Ashaat's malevolent smile filled his mind. He'd kill that scheming snake, make his death long and painful after he forced him to watch his loved ones tortured. Assuming the monster had the propensity to love.

But first, he had to escape. Igtheos had drawn the dagger he always kept strapped to his hip and assumed the flopped limbs and shut eyes of a man still asleep. A skulmor approached the main banquet table he leaned against. Igtheos was quiet, ready, waiting like a spider in the web of bodies. When it got close enough, he'd planned to take it by surprise, then bolt for the door.

Halmand altered his plan, as he often did. When the general came to, he got up in a frenzy, likely smelling the blood as Igtheos had. There was a slight chance the skulmor might have over-looked the commotion of his body thrashing, but there was no missing his scream.

Igtheos had never heard such a cry of anguish. It chilled his blood, pierced his heart like a dagger. He knew what had happened in an instant. Only one thing drew that kind of scream wrenching and writhing from the depths of one's soul: the death of a child.

Right where he'd last made his toast, his tribute to Igtheos and a brighter world, lay Dom, spread out on the table like one of the roasted boars. His throat was torn out, his head cocked at an odd angle as it dangled off the side of the table, eyes rolled back, glassy, mouth ajar. A sword lay on the floor beside him.

Igtheos scarcely got to process his emotions before the skulmor were on them. By some miracle of fury, he and Halmand—along with a handful of rebels who'd awakened from their stupors—rallied and fought their way out of the hall, taking a few skulmor with them. Igtheos bade the surviving rebels to flee. Though loyal, most of them took him up on his offer. They had families and friends elsewhere in the palace, in the city, that they might chance upon before it was too late. Igtheos knew Elize and Zaria were trapped on the upper levels, and he vowed to find them or die in his pursuit. Only Halmand accompanied him, fueled by rage and revenge.

The man had nothing left to lose.

"You don't have to follow me in," Halmand said, drawing Igtheos's attention back to the present. "I can meet you outside."

Igtheos let his silence be the response.

Smoke polluted the hallways as they raced down one after another, the poisonous, heavy air weighing down their lungs. The closer they drew to the feasting hall, the thicker it grew. Halmand barreled on until he reached the gilded double-doors barring the entrance.

"Wait," Igtheos called out, quickening his pace to intercept him. "It's—"

Halmand ignored him and heaved open the doors with enough force to rip one of them off their hinges. Flames jumped out, lashing their golden-red tongues.

A beastly growl emerged from the general as he drew his tunic over his face and leaped through the flames.

Igtheos forced himself to follow. The heat singed his eyebrows as he sprinted after Halmand, but its intensity faded soon after he entered the room. A fire bowl had been spilled over and ignited a tapestry, which spread to another hanging over the doors. Though ash flitted across the room like dark, twisted snowflakes, much of it was left unmarred by the flames, thanks to the stone floor and lack of wooden furniture.

Halmand kneeled over Dom's body. He'd laid the lad on the ground and covered him with his cloak. Halmand wasn't a religious man, but tonight he prayed, hands outstretched to whatever god or goddess might see his son through to the next life.

Igtheos turned to give him privacy. His gaze landed on a small cluster of bodies at the other end of the room. All skulmor. The kills were recent; he and the surviving rebels hadn't killed that many, nor had they fought in that area. He crossed the room, fighting the sense of dread tightening around his stomach like a noose. He froze a few paces away. One body was nyrian—no, human. A waterfall of red hair spilled out from the hood.

Igtheos's knees buckled. He fell to the ground, fingernails scraping the stone as he tensed every muscle in his body to fight off the wave of sobs overtaking him.

No. No, no, no.

Tears blurred his vision as he laid a hand on the tangled mess of red hair. It was matted with blood. Igtheos's thumb grazed the woman's cheek—he couldn't admit it was her, not yet—and found it clammy. He flinched back.

"Gods, no," Halmand said behind him, his voice hoarse. A warm hand blanketed Igtheos's shoulder, squeezed it. "Those fucking monsters."

Igtheos rose, shook his head. He closed his eyes to block out the world. His mind refused to go there, to process what was unfolding. Elize was unstoppable, had protected the mother of all goddesses herself. She survived everything life threw at her, always. She...

No.

Halmand gripped his arm with urgency. "Zaria isn't here."

Igtheos blinked. Zaria. Even now, it was hard to imagine her face instead of Elize's.

"She must have escaped," Halmand continued. "I think... I think Elize sacrificed herself."

A lump formed in Igtheos's throat. Bile swirled in his stomach, threatening to surface.

Halmand clenched his fists. He made a sound more akin to a beast's roar than a man's yell, then stomped on a fallen skulmor's head until it caved in. When he finished, he glanced at Igtheos, his breathing rapid, his face marred with sweat and blood.

"She gave the bastards a fight." Halmand laughed, dark and strained. "I always knew Elize was a warrior in her own right. She must've killed at least four of them. Kicked over that fire pot as a diversion..."

Halmand's consoling words faded into the background as Igtheos studied the blood congealing into the crevices on the stone floor. Darkness ebbed at his vision. He'd always imagined them going together, despite his longevity. Their partnership was more than a marriage, more than friendship. It was a blood pact, two halves of a whole. A memory of her seized his consciousness, pulled him back to a time when life's only worries were court disputes and disputes of their courtship, when they'd sit beside the river, Elize bent over a journal, her lips pinched tightly, while Igtheos reclined beside her, happy to have nothing to do but drink her in.

A muffled cry snapped Igtheos back into the moment, into the suffocating room rank with blood.

"Did you hear that?" Halmand asked, but Igtheos was already stepping over Elize's body, pretending it wasn't hers, it was just some woman's.

The muffled cry sounded louder this time. Clearer.

Igtheos sprinted to the source. Pressed his ear to the wall.

"Mama?" a small voice cried.

Zaria. The secret passage. Igtheos fumbled along the wall until he found the loose stone. He slammed it with his elbow and, once the wall began to slide back, heaved his strength into it to quicken the process.

His daughter lay curled up on the ground, her knees to her chest. She blinked away the light, then, focusing on him, whispered, "Papa?"

Igtheos scooped her up, wrapping his arms around her like a fortress. He wanted to offer words of comfort, tell her that her mother was alright, that she had a plan, as she always did.

Instead, he squeezed her tighter.

Halmand joined them and brushed Zaria's hair back, smiling through tear-stained cheeks. "You beautiful miracle child, you."

Igtheos rose, Zaria still in his arms, and forced himself to resume his role as the leader. "We must rally the remaining survivors and fight our way out of the city. Perhaps we'll even take a few more of them with us. The stormbirds will be back from their hunt at dawn."

Halmand readied his sword in one hand and grabbed the bloodied spear in the other. "We'll see this through yet."

The city burned.

For all Ashaat's talk about the beauty of Cadar, how she was the pride of Nyzar, of Quinaria, with her rolling green fields, detailed architecture, and pristine streets, he hadn't hesitated to sacrifice her for his own gain. They should've seen it coming. Before Elize made off with the scrolls, Ashaat had boasted of the magic contained in them, that they were worth countless lives because they *were* life. Igtheos knew little of the scrolls' capabilities—Elize had sought to protect him from such knowledge—but he no longer questioned their authenticity. Even if their power lay strictly in the wisdom gleaned from years of scholars dissecting the very heart of Quinaria, it was enough to be used as a weapon. Enough to turn a power-hungry leader against his own people.

A lord of ruin is still a lord.

Igtheos heard Ashaat's silken voice say the words as though he whispered in his ear. There was no changing the mind of a man who saw the world as something to be conquered, to be beaten into submission. Some people were born without respect for life, and they were things nightmares were made of.

Halmand elbowed Igtheos as a clicking sound whirred through the air above them. They stole away to the shadow cast by an awning, Zaria's face buried in his neck, just before a monstrous insect hovered by with pincers flexing, eager for its next victim.

Deathstalkers.

It wasn't the first swarm they'd encountered, nor would it be the last. A thick smoke still saturated the air, but it couldn't fully mute the putrid scent of the bugs. They stunk bad enough alive, and the dead, festering ones made his eyes water.

Zaria dug her nails into his exposed arm—he and Halmand hadn't the time to don armor. They'd scarcely cleared the palace alive before sneaking through the courtyard and into the waste drains like skirvin. When they emerged beyond the palace wall, they found bodies strewn everywhere, mostly taken down by skulmor. But as they ventured further into the Sun-blood District, the dead were no longer ravaged with bite marks but littered with arrows and missing limbs hacked away by blades, alluding to the work of Ashaat's soldiers. Because the skulmor and deathstalkers weren't advantage enough.

"Fuck looking for survivors," Halmand hissed once the deathstalker flew out of range. "By now, anyone who was going to escape already has. I say we make for the gates before we count ourselves among the dead."

Igtheos nodded. The only ones worth protecting were right beside him.

"Where's Mama?" Zaria repeated for the dozenth time since clearing the palace. Her eyes were wide, pleading.

Igtheos silenced her with a stern look. He hated himself for it, but he needed her quiet, for her own safety, and theirs. And he couldn't bring himself to tell her that her mother wasn't coming with them, that she'd died, protecting her, when Igtheos needed her alive too. Why hadn't she thought of that instead of being brave? And why in Chai'Tik's name had Ashaat risked killing Elize, his only link to the scrolls?

Because he knew she'd never give them up.

And crushing the rebellion was all the cause he needed.

"Igtheos." Halmand grabbed him firmly by the shoulders and shook him. Hard. "I need you to focus. I'm taking the alleyways to the trade gates, and you're coming with me. Otherwise, I'll take that precious bundle and leave you here to die. Do you understand?"

Igtheos tightened his grip on Zaria. He marched past Halmand, almost tripping over a body in the alleyway. His movements were stiff, awkward, as though his muscles were taxed from days of fighting. But the fight had only just begun.

He clenched his teeth together and jogged down the narrow pathway, rounding the corner ahead of Halmand, his source of protection, as his arms wielded Zaria instead of a weapon.

Something with the strength of an armored horse smacked him to the ground. His head knocked against the stone path. The crackles of flames and shouts from Halmand dulled as a loud ringing filled his ears. He distantly registered Zaria slipping from his grasp.

Spiney legs scrabbled at Igtheos, scraping the sides of his arms as the deathstalker straddled him and raised its venom-tipped stinger above its head. Despite the heat from the nearby flames, a chill ran down his back. He retrieved his dagger, drove it into the soft section of its underside, where its armored abdomen connected with its thorax. A weak link. The deathstalker hissed and brought its pincers down on Igtheos's neck, but not before he drove the dagger into its jaws. He kicked it off, and the wolf-sized insect slammed into the side of a building with a *crunch*. Igtheos scarcely had time to unsheathe his sword before another was on him. He hacked off its wing with two swift strikes, then spun and delivered the final blow to the one crumpled against the wall. He could faintly make out the form of Halmand fighting beside him, the general's war cries loud and mighty.

A sharp pain stabbed Igtheos's thigh. He lunged and hacked at the bug's head until it was ripped away from its body. An oozy goo seeped from the cavity and pooled into a foul-smelling puddle at his feet. He staggered back and glanced at the sky, sword drawn and ears attuned to the telltale buzzing, but no other deathstalkers lurked nearby. He looked down at his throbbing leg and breathed a sigh of relief: he'd only been bitten. He'd survive, unlike those who suffered a sting. There was no coming back from a deathstalker's poison.

Igtheos tore off a piece of his tunic and tied it around his thigh to slow the bleeding. He searched the alleyway. Halmand leaned against the side of a house, panting. Zaria...

A tightness seized Igtheos's chest, as though cold, grasping claws squeezed the air out of him. He couldn't move. Couldn't breathe. Blackness ebbed at his vision; his mind was a hurricane of sheer terror. He opened his mouth to call her name, but no sound came out. Numbly, he willed his legs forward, searching among the fallen deathstalkers for her petite body. He dashed down the alleyway, limbs moving on their own. Halmand raced after him, screaming Zaria's name until his voice went horse from exertion. No longer caring who saw him, Igtheos rerouted to the main road where he kicked down doors, leaped over bodies, and rushed through flames.

He cut down another deathstalker. Some of Ashaat's soldiers. At least five, maybe ten. He lost count of the heads he lopped off, the chests he pierced, the screams he cut short. They were mere obstacles. Dead wood to cut through. Soulless underlings blindly following a monster who told them their lives mattered more than everyone else's. They'd pay for their allegiance.

At some point, Igtheos's body gave out, and he found himself kneeling in a puddle of blood tainted with deathstalker gel. Dawn marred the sky with the same bloodied colors staining the city. The ground was cool against his cheek. He inhaled a sickening scent of blood and ash. The scent of death.

This was death *before* death, when everyone around you died first, when it should've been you all along. The gods could have him now. There was nothing left to live for.

Halmand's sandaled feet stood inches from his face, shifting anxiously. He kneeled beside Igtheos, his fingers curling and uncurling, almost reaching out and then drawing back, as though he knew his comfort mattered not.

Igtheos opened his mouth to tell him to go, that there was no more rebellion, no point in saving the scraps of his soul, when an avian shriek pierced the air. A shadow fell over him, then the road trembled with the intensity of a groundshake.

Araynia.

The stormbird let out another cry, and thunder rumbled in the distance, followed closely by the crackle of lightning, calling the rest of the flock to her.

Her presence stoked the last surviving ember of Igtheos's spirit, igniting it into a pyre of rage as wild as the flames that decimated the city. With a grunt, he drew his legs beneath him to stand and looked up at the roof Araynia had perched atop, her taloned feet covering the entirety of the house. He climbed up to her, ready to take to the skies. Elize and Zaria's memory would live on, and he'd take his vengeance, even if it killed him. Ashaat and his men would get the same mercy they showed the rebels.

Tonight, the war would end.

EPILOGUE

Igtheos pulled the mask down tighter on his face. Icy wind cut through his clothes, raising the hairs on his arms and awakening the shriveled remnants of his soul. The air in Neharem was pure, untainted by the stench of industry, its forests full and thriving, its waterways pure, its creatures flourishing. From above, there was little to hint at the presence of non-beast life. Not so much as a large structure, and certainly no land cleared for great cities.

The eye holes in his mask made for somewhat obstructed viewing, but it was better than the blurred tears he'd suffered otherwise. He urged Araynia closer to the tree line, hoping to catch a glimpse of civilization below. According to Elize's travel log, the Apáasutai would be more welcoming than the tribes they'd encountered so far. The ones who'd received the surviving rebels when they'd first washed ashore half-starved and dehydrated, the Kahaloán, weren't necessarily volatile, but nor were they eager to have their new guests stay long. Not long after they cleared the coastal tribe's territory, they'd crossed paths with the Lautei, a nyrian-dominant people who saw little reason to let their intruders live. It had taken all of Igtheos's peace-bringing skills and, finally, a show of their surviving warriors' weapons and the ferocity of their two stormbirds to grant them safe passage. He didn't doubt they would've faced a far different fate without the latter.

Araynia's feathers ruffled as they glided over the sea of green. The trees grew thicker the closer they got to Neharem's northwestern coast, their colors vibrant, the branches obstructing any view of the ground and the life nestled within. And there, a glimmer of coastline. The stormbird saw it too—she'd likely noticed quite a ways' back before Igtheos even registered it—and arced in that direction, her midnight blue wings cutting through the dawn like a paintbrush.

Igtheos pressed his face into Araynia's massive, feathered neck, and the smell of rain and musk filled his senses, bringing a wave of peace. It wasn't long, however, before visions of Elize usurped his thoughts, followed by the rest of that fateful, bloodied night. He didn't think he'd ever forget any of it, as much as he wished he could.

And Zaria... he'd been slow to accept the likely outcome of her fate, that she'd been carried off by deathstalkers, torn apart by skulmor, or captured by Ashaat's men. None would've left her alive. If by some miracle she had been brought before Ashaat...

Igtheos refused to think on it. He'd wish death upon her a dozen times before imagining her in the hands of a man who sought to eradicate her kind.

He'd given everything to find her that night. Araynia called down the lightning, and its sparks intensified the fire, driving the deathstalkers back into the mountains they called home. Belmond, her mate, made similar work of the palace grounds, and the skulmor were soon racing through the streets, easy prey for Araynia and the small band of surviving rebels rallied around Halmand. But no matter how long they searched, there was no sign of Zaria. Not even the stormbirds' impeccable vision could locate her among the living. Or dead. Some part of Igtheos was glad they never found a body, for no body meant no surety of death, and in his dreams, he could imagine her not just surviving, but thriving. A larger part of him also knew they'd never be reunited again, at least not in this life.

Igtheos would've kept up his search, unsatisfied until every inch of the city had been inspected for signs of his daughter, but Ashaat's army had soon raised the gates and began picking off survivors. Araynia took several arrows to the chest, and Igtheos reluctantly guided her down to collect Halmand and his band of rebels while Belmond retrieved some more. The city looked oddly peaceful as they soared over it, the flames subsiding into warm, glowing embers resembling the tranquility of a hearth. He couldn't see the bodies from that high up, but he knew they were there, left alone and in pain as they transitioned between worlds, if such hope awaited them. Igtheos wasn't sure he wished for life to continue beyond the one promised. What good was it to experience pain over again, to chase your wildest dreams, to love unconditionally, if it mattered not in the end?

Because you loved, and you lived. And isn't that enough, my darling? To think that of all the beings throughout the great expanse of time, you were lucky enough to breathe in this moment, to cast a ripple in the water?

Igtheos couldn't recall if those were the exact words Elize had once spoken to him or if he'd fabricated them out of her very essence, but they were her beliefs, and he'd cling to them until the end of his days.

Araynia took an abrupt dive, jolting Igtheos back to the bitter present, and with a thunderous shake, the noble bird secured a perch on a cliff overlooking the sea. To his left was the Khitamic Ocean, strikingly calm and welcoming in contrast to the jagged rockface its waves crashed upon. To the right, a forest rich with life, dark yet welcoming, and hauntingly quiet. Igtheos dismounted—a task he once found precarious, but now he slid down the stormbird's feathers and landed on the ground with some semblance of grace—and marched toward the woods. Araynia shrieked in protest.

"I'm fine, my friend," Igtheos told her. "You should hunt, fill your belly with enough whale to share with your mate. You must look out for him, for yourself. I can't lose you, too." His voice was unsteady, wavering with a deep emotion he couldn't put into words.

Araynia's golden eyes widened, then closed. She curled her neck down into her chest as if considering the weight of his words. Igtheos knew she felt it too, the guilt. Like him, she was the leader of her flock, the guardian of the last stormbirds, and she'd let them down. Not that she could've done much more than she had. From what he'd pieced together after hearing the accounts of survivors near the coastline, the stormbirds were hunting when Ashaat's plan unfurled, and while Igtheos's rebels weathered the land attacks of skulmor and deathstalkers and compliant, unquestioning soldiers, the sea unleashed a terror all its own. Ashaat had somehow persuaded some myrem, sea-dwellers who'd scarcely been seen in centuries, to join him in his cause. And loyal to them were seaserpents, the sinewy monsters of the deep, wildest and most powerful of the Great Beasts of Old.

Araynia and her flock would've been no match for them, not unprepared. The seaserpents must've sprang from the water and snatched the birds from the sky, one by one, dragging them down into a watery grave. Only Araynia and her mate, Belmond, had survived. How any myrem could partake in the cold-blooded murder of stormbirds, magnificent creatures already facing extinction, was beyond Igtheos's reckoning. Unless they feared something even more powerful than themselves. He'd never know. Chai'Tik herself couldn't drag him back to his homeland now.

Igtheos placed a hand on Araynia's curved beak. It could crush his entire body in an instant, swallow him whole. But he had no fear. He gave respect where it was due, and Araynia could sense it. She butted his chest gently, then flapped her great wings, causing the loose rock and dirt from the cliffside to swirl around him.

And she was gone.

Igtheos felt eyes on him long before the first Apáasutai made an appearance. He'd pegged his first stalker shortly after entering the dense undergrowth of the forest, and by the time he'd walked half a mile through grasping branches and over fallen logs, at least two more pursued him. He chose to play ignorant. Best to let his would-be captors assume him unaware and incapable of self-defense. It made him less of a threat, and, perhaps, someone they'd be more likely to consider helping.

He feigned surprise when his pursuers emerged from a cluster of ferns, spears lowered and defenses high. Two women, three men, all garbed in elaborately woven, blanket-like cloaks of bold colors with leather leggings beneath. The women were nyrian with braided white hair and ashen violet skin. Two of the men were human, their dark-hair also braided, and the last was another nyrian, his skin a russet-brown, his eyes a deep red, vibrant and illuminated in the forest's shade. He carried a staff instead of a spear, which was the only material evidence signaling to Igtheos that he was indeed in charge. Not that the man needed it. The way he carried himself, the wisdom in his eyes, the steadiness of his hand—it was all enough to command respect.

He approached Igtheos, raised an eyebrow. *"Itchowna."*

Igtheos spread his arms to show he wasn't a threat, was unarmed, and shook his head no, he didn't understand, didn't speak whatever language the locals had evolved to use over the millennia they'd been in Neharem. The leader was nyrian, like Igtheos. Perhaps there was a chance some of his distant kin had retained their mother language. Igtheos dared a step closer and touched his chest.

"Igtheos," he said calmly.

Understanding washed over the nyrian leader's face. He touched his own chest with a wrinkled but strong hand. "Elenathor."

"Do you speak the first language of our kin?" Igtheos asked. "Nyrinian?"

Elenathor's expression was unreadable. Igtheos pressed on, more out of desperation than hope. Perhaps his body language would convey enough.

"My people and I have come to Neharem seeking refuge," he explained. "We've suffered through a great deal of injustice and war, and we're few in number and weak in spirit. We don't seek charity, only community. If you lend us aid, in time we'll repay you tenfold. I swear. I'm a man of my word. It's..." Igtheos's throat constricted as he fought back the rage-tinged sadness swelling within him. "It's all I have left."

A warrior gestured at Igtheos with his spear and muttered something to Elenathor. Igtheos's hand found its way to the hilt of the dagger fastened to his belt, and he lightly drummed it with his fingertips.

"You ride with the mother of birds," Elenathor said, holding his warriors back with his twisted staff. His Nyrinian was rough and laden with a foreign accent, but the knowledge was there, and it served as a bridge between them. "All my life I thought they were myth, a child's dream. I want to meet her. Pay her respect."

Igtheos twisted the singed edges of his tunic. "She's not mine to command, but I'm happy to ask her."

That answer seemed to satisfy Elenathor, who nodded and beckoned Igtheos closer. "How many are you?"

"Fewer than three hundred." *And once greater than three thousand.* His chest tightened with the weight of the thought, as though a boulder pressed down upon him.

"You have many stormbirds in your company?"

"Only two."

The nyrian's eyes narrowed, as if deciding whether to trust his response. Then he turned abruptly and, without looking back, commanded, "Walk with me."

They followed a well-trodden path through the forest, their leather-wrapped feet compressing the humus and swiftly navigating around even the smallest of plant life. Igtheos swore he'd never smelled air so alive. It brimmed with the must of soil, the bite of coniferous trees, the briny ocean wind. As they walked, one of the women smiled at him, offered her waterskin. Igtheos accepted the gift and raised it to his lips. Crystalline water poured in, alive and pure. Elize would've liked it, he thought. Maybe she'd even tasted this exact water from this source on her quest to hide the scrolls. He quickened his pace to catch up with Elenathor. Asking would only bring him more pain, but he had to know.

"Have you encountered another newcomer within the last few moon cycles?" he asked, his fingernails digging into his palms. "A woman, human, hair red as the sky at sunset?"

Elenathor shook his head. "You are the first visitor in my lifetime."

Igtheos's heart sank. He didn't intend to go searching for the scrolls; the wretched things should never be found. But simply knowing one was nearby would've brought him some peace, as though there were a small part of Elize left to protect.

He vowed to never let his hope flourish again.

The smell of smoked fish was the first sign of a settlement, followed by voices, and soon after, Igtheos found himself gazing into a clearing surrounded by the tallest trees he'd ever seen. Their trunks seemed to stretch up for miles, and he immediately got the sense that the place was sacred. Several long, wooden houses made up the small village, and adults and children alike puttered about, tending to the daily activities that occupied the Apáasutai people. Some busied themselves with woodworking, while others wove blankets, cooked meals, or hung herbs to dry. A group of children squealed with delight as an elderly man led them in a game of sticks and wooden hoops, chasing after him like a flock of ducklings. In the center of the village roared a large fire, and Igtheos found himself drawn to it, to the people.

"What do you call this?" he asked Elenathor. He hesitated just outside the clearing, not daring to step foot into the village until invited.

"*Agaas.*" Elenathor brushed his hand across one of the massive tree trunks. "It is the Apáasutai word for peace, and it is what we strive to bring to this land. Long have the tribes of Neharem been at war with each other. My mother, former chief of the Apáasutai, dreamed we'd one day be united, for she had visions of a time when outsiders would come and lay claim to the land."

"I'm not one of those men," Igtheos said, perhaps too quickly.

Elenathor offered a sad sort of smile. "I don't think you are. But you are proof that it will happen. Your land is beginning to sour, and it is only a matter of time before more of your kind spread like a plague. It may be thousands of years still, but it will happen. And right now, my people aren't prepared to deal with such a threat."

Igtheos kneeled before Elenathor and bowed his head. "Then I will help you in whatever way I can. Take us in, and we will honor your ways. I will tell you all you wish to know about my homeland and assist you in uniting yours. We could make this a great nation."

"We are already a great nation." Elenathor gestured to his people, to the trees. "And we are not yet so hardened of heart to turn you away. Come, bring your people to Agaas, and we will see what beauty can rise from the ashes of your loss."

Igtheos gripped Elenathor's arm, only considering after the fact that he might perceive the gesture as threatening. But the elder nyrian smiled and gripped Igtheos's arm tighter in return.

"I am forever indebted to you," Igtheos said. "You will not regret this."

"Life is too short for regret. I choose to not make room for it. Something tells me you'd be wise to implement a similar way of being."

Igtheos remained at the edge of the clearing as Elenathor and the warriors greeted their loved ones. No regrets? He regretted every moment of his life up to this one, for they'd led him here, a failure, a murderer, a widower, and childless. He swallowed, clenched and unclenched his fists, fighting the memories with every inch of his being. But there were good ones, too, buried beneath the grief, and though he regretted recent events, he cherished countless moments prior, all that beauty woven into the pain.

And it *was* worth it.

He ventured into the clearing with hesitant steps. A wooden hoop rolled to a stop and flopped before his feet, and a young girl trailed it, gazing up at Igtheos in wide-eyed wonder. He kneeled to retrieve the hoop, then offered it to her. The girl flashed a smile and scampered back to her friends, beckoning them to come see the newcomer who lingered at the edge of their woods.

A warmth spread through Igtheos's chest, and for the first time since that fateful night, he felt he'd found something to live for.

"Do you see, Elize?" he whispered quietly enough that only he'd hear. "I'm here, like you wanted, fighting for what's right no matter the cost. I hope this helps you and Zaria live on, even if it's just a ghost of a memory. I'll trust the river to take me where it may."

And trust it, he did.

AUTHOR'S NOTE

Thank you for reading *From the Ashes*. If this was your first foray into Quinaria, I hope it whetted your appetite for the rest of the series, and if you've already read *Of Thieves and Shadows*, I promise there's more coming soon.

If you can spare a few minutes, I'd be ever so honored if you left a review on Goodreads and Amazon. Aside from purchasing a book, leaving a rating and review is one of the best ways to support an author. Your feedback is important to me and will help other readers both find the book and decide whether to read it.

While I'm assuming you came into possession of this story via my newsletter sign-up, there's the off-chance you purchased the paperback instead. If that's the case, signing up at www.bshgarcia.com will provide you exclusive access to monthly updates on my writing journey, upcoming releases, ARC opportunities, and advanced viewings of covers, snippets, and blurbs. And who knows when I might toss up a deleted chapter or free short story just for the hell of it?

You can also interact with me on Instagram and Twitter (@bshgarcia), and follow me for important updates on Facebook, Goodreads, and Threads (same handle).

Thank you again for your support. I can't wait to thrust you into the next installment of this epic saga.

–B. S. H. Garcia

ACKNOWLEDGMENTS

Even a story this short (yes, 16.5k words *is*, in fact, short... to me) requires many eyes on the paper and many hands on the keyboard.

I'm forever indebted to my early readers and critique partners, specifically Jared, Kelsey, and Kaylea. You all know how to mix the right amount of critical feedback with compliments—except you, Jared. Never got the whole sandwich feedback structure down, did you? Still, your questions and hole-picking are invaluable. Kelsey and Kaylea, you are always there when I need you, dedicating your precious time to my stories and characters, quick to read and thorough in your reflections. I hope you never leave me. Oh, wait, you can't. I wrote it into the fine print of the last document you critiqued.

[insert maniacal laugh here]

Björn and Éowyn, thanks for tolerating so much Gravity Falls, Bluey, and Miss Rachel so I could get my work done. I don't always find the perfect balance between parenting and work, but you give me endless grace and love. And sleepless nights. So, we're even.

Thank you to my editor, Jon, especially for squeezing me in last-minute so I could meet deadlines. Your care and attention to detail is a rarity, and I'm honored to work with you.

To everyone who's supported me from the earliest days of this dream, thank you. There are too many of you across too many platforms, but know that every comment, every message, every time you share my story with the world or write some kind words about it, it makes my day. Literally. I do the majority of my work in isolation, just me and my crazy mind. But when I see someone touched by my writing, be that a social media post or a full-length novel, it makes this passion worthwhile. I mean, I'd probably still do it anyway because I'm a psycho with voices in my head that need to be released via storytelling or else I'll starting miming in the street... BUT I'd much rather write for you.

As always, thank you, dear reader. Life is short, time is precious, and you gave me a small part of that. I can never thank you enough for choosing to spend time with my stories, and I hope it was worth your while.

Much love.

ABOUT THE AUTHOR

B. S. H. Garcia is the author of the epic fantasy series, *The Heart of Quinaria*. A household manager by day, writer by night, she graduated with honors from The University of Colorado with a bachelor's degree in English Writing. To get into character for her stories, she trudges through the woods in cosplay with a mead-filled drinking horn and has traveled from Oregon to New Zealand seeking inspiration. Visit her online at www.bs hgarcia.com.